This Ladybird Book belongs to:

This Ladybird retelling
by
Sampurna Chatterjee

Published by Penguin Books India
11 Community Centre, Panchsheel Park, New Delhi 110017

1 3 5 7 9 10 8 6 4 2

Printed in Ajanta Offset & Packagings Ltd., New Delhi

FAVOURITE TALES

Riki Tiki Tavi

illustrated
by
RAMEN SARKAR

based on a story by Rudyard Kipling

Riki Tiki Tavi was a mongoose. His nose was pink. His eyes were sharp. His tail was like a brush. And his cry was loud, 'Riki-tik-tiki-tiki-tchck!'

One day, a flood swept Riki Tiki out of his burrow and washed him into a little ditch, where he fainted.

When he woke up, the sun was shining, and a little boy was saying, 'Look! A little mongoose! Let's take him home and look after him.'

Riki Tiki was carried into a big house. The little boy, Teddy, wrapped him in cotton wool and he felt warm and cold at once, and sneezed, 'AAACHHOO!'

Teddy gave Riki Tiki a piece of meat, which he ate hungrily. Feeling better, he ran around the table.

Then Riki Tiki climbed onto Teddy's shoulder. Teddy took Riki Tiki to the sunny veranda, where he dried his fur, and thought about his new home. 'Run and find out,' his parents had always told him. And that's exactly what Riki Tiki did.

He ran and found the bathtub, and nearly drowned. He found a bottle of ink and got an inky nose. He ran into Teddy's bed and when Teddy's parents came in to say goodnight, they found Riki Tiki on the pillow.

'What if he bites Teddy?' Mother said.

'He won't,' said Father. 'He'll guard Teddy with his life. Now, if a snake…'

But Mother refused to even listen to another word about snakes!

In the morning, Riki Tiki went out into the garden to go where his twitchy little nose led him. It was a huge garden! There were roses, sweet-smelling lime and orange trees, green bamboo and wavy high grass.

Riki Tiki thought, 'I'm going to have such fun hunting here!'

Just then, he heard the saddest sound in the world. Darzee, the tailorbird, and his wife were weeping. 'Booo-hoo-hoo!' they cried, as they sat on a tree by their beautiful nest.

'What's wrong?' Riki Tiki asked them.

'Our baby fell out of the nest and Nag ate him!'

'I'm sorry,' said Riki Tiki. 'But who's Nag?'

Instead of answering, Darzee and his wife vanished.

From the grass
below the thorn
bush where the
nest was, came
a low sound that
made Riki Tiki
jump.

Hisssssss!

Out of the grass, inch
by slimy inch, came a
long, thick cobra. He lifted
himself up and swayed above Riki Tiki,
his cold eyes black and deadly.

'Who isss Nag?' he hissed. 'I am! Look
and be ssscared!'

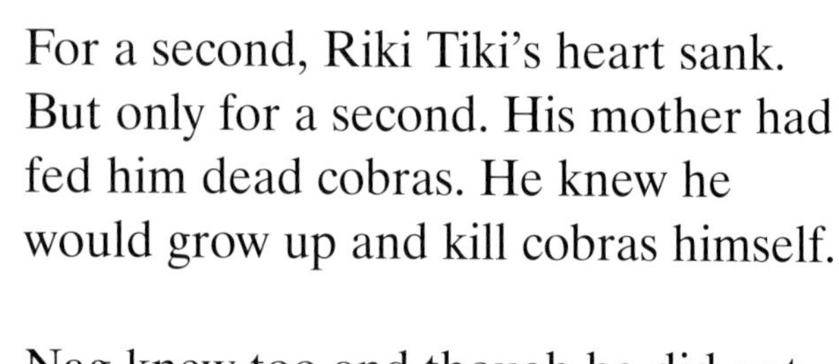

For a second, Riki Tiki's heart sank. But only for a second. His mother had fed him dead cobras. He knew he would grow up and kill cobras himself.

Nag knew too and though he did not show it, he was afraid.

'Very grand!' said Riki Tiki, boldly. 'But why eat little baby birds?'

‘Why not?’ said Nag, calmly. ‘You eat eggsss, do you not?’

‘Watch out!’ shrieked Darzee suddenly. ‘Behind you!’

Riki Tiki jumped. With an angry hiss, a huge snake’s head whizzed under him. It was Nagina, Nag’s wife.

While he had been talking, she had crept up from behind.

Riki Tiki leapt on Nagina, and bit her, but not hard enough. She slithered away, bleeding. Nag, too, disappeared.

Riki Tiki's eyes were red. He was angry and excited. But now he had to get serious. He had to…

'Look out!' a tiny voice snapped.

It was Karait, the dusty brown snake, small and very poisonous. Riki Tiki didn't care. Proud at having escaped Nagina, he jumped on Karait, bit him neatly and killed him.

‘Mother! Father! Our mongoose is killing a snake!’ Teddy called out. ‘Come quick!’

By the time Father came running up with a stick, Karait was already dead.

Riki Tiki was kissed, praised and petted all through dinner. It was only when Teddy fell asleep that Riki Tiki got a chance to slip away. In the dark, he bumped into Chuchundra, the muskrat.

‘Be careful, Riki Tiki!’ Chuchundra said, fearfully.

‘Why?’ said Riki Tiki.

‘No one is safe with Nag around!’ Chuchundra wailed. ‘And now he has a nest full of eggs, and soon there will be many cobras all over.’

‘Nag is in the garden,’ said Riki Tiki.

'No. Listen!' said Chuchundra.

Riki Tiki heard the faint scritch-scratch of a snake's scales sliding over dry bricks. 'Nag!' he thought. 'Crawling in through the bathroom pipe!'

He ran to the bathroom and listened. ‘When the man and his family are dead, the mongoossse will have to go away,’ Nagina whispered outside.

‘Mussst we kill them all?’ Nag hissed back.

‘Yesss! When they were not here, were there any mongoossses? No! Go! Kill whoever comesss in!’

Riki Tiki saw Nag slide in, curl himself around the big bucket and fall asleep.

An hour passed.

Slowly, barely breathing, Riki Tiki crept towards Nag. 'I must bite the head,' he thought desperately. 'Bite above the hood and not let go.'

Riki Tiki jumped on Nag's neck and bit. In a second Nag was up and shaking his head from side to side. Riki Tiki hit the bathtub and the wall again and again. Every bone ached. His head spun. His eyes were shut as tight as his teeth. 'I'll die,' he thought, 'but at least I'll die fighting.'

BANG!

Father's gun went off. Nag stopped moving and Riki Tiki let go, ready to roll over and die. But he was not dead. A little dizzy perhaps, but alive!

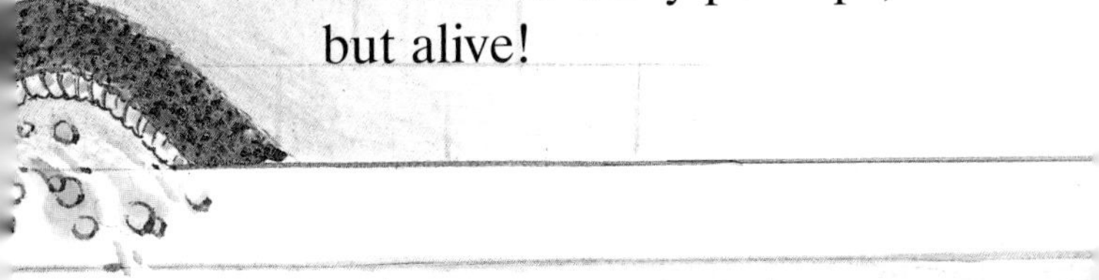

Next morning, Darzee was singing at the top of his voice. 'Nag the snake is dead-dead-dead. Riki Tiki Tavi bit off his head-head-head!'

'Darzee, tell me where Nagina is!' Riki Tiki said.

'Near the rubbish-heap-heap-heap!' Darzee sang. 'Tonight we can sleep-sleep-sleep.'

'Where are her eggs?' Riki Tiki asked.

'Near the melon bed-bed-bed, oh….'

'Darzee,' Riki said, 'pretend to have a broken wing and draw Nagina away.'

Darzee was too happy to listen. But his wife flew out to the rubbish heap and fluttered about, moaning, ‘Oh my wing! I can’t fly!’

Nagina started slithering towards the bird.

Riki Tiki ran to the melon bed. There were twenty-five eggs which would soon hatch into twenty-five little cobras. He crushed the eggs, one by one.

When three were left he heard Darzee's wife screaming: 'Riki Tiki!'

He broke two more and, carrying the third egg in his mouth, ran towards the house. There he stopped. On the veranda, a few inches away from Teddy's bare leg, was Nagina, poised to strike.

'Turn around, Nagina!' Riki Tiki shouted. 'Turn and fight me!'

'Later, Riki Tiki. Now, weep for your friendsss!'

'Weep for your last egg, Nagina!' Riki Tiki shouted. 'Look!'

Nagina spun around. Immediately, Father pulled Teddy to his side, safe.

Riki Tiki danced around Nagina, out of reach. She lashed out and, each time, he leapt away. He dropped the egg. In a flash, Nagina had it in her mouth. She flew across the garden and into her hole at the base of the melon bush. Riki Tiki plunged in after her.

Dark. Silence. Above ground, Darzee began to cry. Even grown mongooses didn't dare to follow a snake into its hole all alone.

Just then, Riki Tiki Tavi crept out of the hole, muddy and sore. He looked around, curled up and fell asleep.

That night, Riki Tiki feasted on all the good things that Teddy's family gave him to eat. 'Very nice, but what's all the fuss about?' Riki Tiki thought. 'I was doing my job!'